THE SECRET EXPLORERS
AND THE JURASSIC RESCUE

CONTENTS

Chapter One
JOURNEY TO THE JURASSIC

Tamiko shuffled along the beach on her hands and knees. The sharp pebbles dug into her skin, but she hardly noticed. She was focused on her favorite thing—hunting for fossils! There were millions of them mixed in with the sand and seaweed of Nemuro beach, where she lived in Japan. But spotting them was hard, and you had to concentrate.

Tamiko sifted through the sand with her fingers. The sharp edge of a stone caught her eye.

"Ha!" she said.

Tamiko lifted the stone from its sandy bed and brushed it clean. It was an ammonite fossil! She'd known as soon as she saw its spiral shell. Ammonites were sea creatures that had lived at the same time as the dinosaurs. They were related to the octopus and squid that swam in the oceans today.

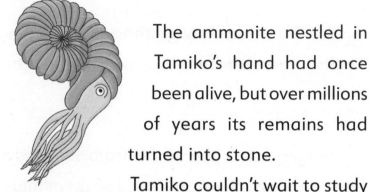

The ammonite nestled in Tamiko's hand had once been alive, but over millions of years its remains had turned into stone.

Tamiko couldn't wait to study her new treasure. She put the ammonite in her pocket and strolled home, passing tourists who'd come to see the small beachside town. She paused outside her favorite shop and gazed through the large window. Inside was a glittering display of crystals and semiprecious stones. The shop had fossils for sale, too, which were kept in a case at the back.

But something else caught her eye. On the shop door was a glowing compass symbol! A thrill ran through Tamiko. Her hand went to the matching compass badge on her T-shirt. The compass was the symbol for the Secret Explorers.

"Looks like we've got a new mission!" she said.

Taking a deep breath, Tamiko opened the shop door. But instead of the usual glass cases full of crystals and fossils, Tamiko walked into a dazzling white light. A strong wind whipped her short black hair around her head. She felt as if she was flying—and then the light faded.

Spots were dancing in her eyes and Tamiko blinked them away. She was back in the Exploration Station! She grinned with delight as she took in the familiar room. It had rows of humming computer screens set into the black stone walls. There were display cases here too, just like the ones in the Nemuro fossil shop. They were full of meteorites, shells and other finds from previous missions. The domed ceiling had a huge picture of the stars and planets of Milky Way, and on the floor was a huge map of the world.

Tamiko was the first to arrive.

"Tamiko—reporting for duty!" she said aloud to the Exploration Station, before settling down in one of the comfy chairs.

It wasn't long before the

other Secret Explorers appeared in the glowing doorway.

"Leah—here!" said a tall girl with a bright smile, saluting as she always did. She had a smudge of earth on her cheek.

"Been gardening, Leah?" Tamiko asked with a grin. Leah was the Biology Explorer, and knew everything about plants and animals.

Leah looked proudly at her muddy fingernails. "You know it, Tamiko!"

Kiki, the Engineering Explorer, was next. She pushed her glasses onto her nose. "Kiki—here!" she said.

"Ollie—here!" said a red-haired boy. In his hands he was holding a magazine about the Amazon River. Ollie was the Rainforest Explorer.

"Roshni—here!" said a girl with long dark hair tied up in a ponytail. As the Space Explorer, Roshni knew all about stars, planets, and galaxies.

"Connor—here!" Connor's hair was wet. It looked like the Marine Explorer had been investigating the aquatic life he loved.

A boy holding a book about the Aztecs came through. "Gustavo—here!" said the History Explorer.

The last member of the team arrived. "Cheng—here!"

Tamiko grinned at Cheng, the Geology Explorer. Cheng's love of rocks meant they had a lot to talk about.

They gathered around the huge floor map that showed the world. The map

usually glowed in the spot where the mission would take place. But something else happened this time.

"Hey!" said Tamiko in surprise. "Is it me, or is the map... moving?"

The continents were shifting around, sliding and bumping into each other. As the Secret Explorers watched, the world changed

shape completely. Instead of Africa, Antarctica, Asia, Australia, Europe, North America, and South America, there were just two big continents.

"That's what the world looked like during the Jurassic Period," said Cheng. "One hundred and fifty million years ago!"

The Secret Explorers exchanged excited glances. It looked like two of them were going to travel back to the time of the dinosaurs! *I hope it's me*, Tamiko thought. I would love to see actual living dinosaurs!

A screen appeared in the area of land that would one day be central Europe. It glowed and expanded. The screen showed a leafy background and a roundish, white object. Tamiko stared at it in wonder.

"It's a dinosaur egg!" she exclaimed. "Maybe our mission is to protect it."

The Exploration Station always picked two Secret Explorers for each mission. Tamiko crossed her fingers. She looked down at her chest... and sure enough, her compass badge was glowing.

"All RIGHT!" she said with a whoop. "I'm in!"

Cheng's badge lit up. "Me too!" he said.

Gustavo grinned. "A Dinosaur Explorer and a Geology Explorer," he said. "The perfect combination for a mission to the Jurassic! The Exploration Station always knows who to choose."

Cheng exchanged an excited high-five with Tamiko.

Kiki headed to a big red button on the wall. She pushed it and a battered old go-kart called the Beagle rose out of the floor. It didn't look like much, but it wasn't named after Charles Darwin's famous exploration ship for nothing. There was more to the Beagle than met the eye...

The other Secret Explorers took their places at the computer terminals, ready to give Tamiko and Cheng any help they needed on their mission.

"Good luck, guys," said Ollie.

"Don't get eaten by a T. rex!" said Leah.

"Tyrannosaurus rex lived during the Cretaceous Period, which came after the Jurassic," Tamiko reassured her. "But we'll definitely be careful!"

Tamiko and Cheng climbed into the

Beagle and sat down. Tamiko took the wobbly steering wheel.

"Ready when you are," said Cheng with a nod.

Tamiko pressed the "START" button. The Beagle began to shake and rattle, like it was hurtling down a very steep hill. Tamiko held on tight.

There was a blinding flash of light and the Exploration Station disappeared. The steering wheel transformed beneath Tamiko's hands into a sturdy set of handlebars, and the old seats became deep and comfortable.

There was a splash and the light faded. Tamiko blinked. She and Cheng were now wearing helmets, and she was holding on to the handlebars of a chunky quad bike. Its wheels were half-submerged in a murky green swamp. On the banks, trees with delicate leaves drooped over the water and bright green ferns sprouted from the soil. Strange sounds filled the air. Everything smelled earthy and different.

"Check out this place!" said Cheng.

A whirring sound overhead made Tamiko duck. She felt the whoosh of air as a creature with vast leathery wings flew right over the top of their heads.

"Wow," she breathed. It was a Klobiodon— a type of enormous pterosaur! It opened its long beak, revealing sharp teeth, and screeched.

Tamiko grinned at Cheng. "Welcome to the Jurassic!"

Chapter Two
STEGOSAURUS RESCUE

"This is unbelievable!" Cheng said. The pterosaur flew high above them, soaring on its gigantic wings. "We've gone back one hundred and fifty million years, Tamiko!"

Around the edges of the swamp grew big plants called cycads, which looked a bit like palm trees with very thick trunks. Among them were tall, graceful ginkgo trees with clusters of yellow fruit. There were conifers with dark, feathery branches, and bright green ferns with curling leaves. Strange dinosaur calls were coming from all around them. Tamiko listened excitedly to the faint croaks, deep grunts, and a big, booming cry.

A clump of ferns rustled. Cheng clutched Tamiko's sleeve in surprise as a group of turkey-sized dinosaurs burst out and sprinted along the bank. They had long athletic legs and fluffy orange-pink bellies.

"What are those?" he asked.

"Compsognathus," said Tamiko. "They must be hunting something! They're running really fast, aren't they?"

As the Compsognathuses hurtled out of sight, the Beagle suddenly rocked from side to side. *BEEP BRRRP BARPP!* it squeaked in alarm.

"Whoa!" cried Tamiko.

Beside her, Cheng gripped the seat. Something was bumping against the Beagle. Something in the swamp...

Tamiko peered into the murky green water. She saw four huge flippers and a very long neck.

The creature bumped into the side of the Beagle, and it rocked again.

"Is it a crocodile?" asked Cheng nervously.

"A plesiosaur," Tamiko said. "Plesiosaurs lived in the seas and swamps. I think it's just checking us out." She laughed. "It's never seen a quad bike before!"

The plesiosaur lifted its head from the water. Tamiko caught a flash of teeth in a huge, yawning mouth. This wasn't quite so funny anymore.

"We should drive to the shore before it knocks us into the swamp," she said. "Come on!" She twisted the throttle on the Beagle's handlebars. The engine roared, and the

wheels started turning. They drove onto the shore and parked the Beagle beneath a large ginkgo tree.

"We'd better start searching for that dinosaur egg," Cheng said as they climbed off the quad bike and hung their helmets on its handlebars. "But how will we know where to look?"

Tamiko pictured the egg the Exploration Station had shown them. It had looked so delicate and vulnerable. "Let's go up onto higher ground," she suggested. "If we can see where we are, maybe we'll get a clue about where to start searching."

They set off through the trees. Some way

in the distance, Tamiko saw a herd of quietly grazing Cetiosauruses. They reached up with their long necks to nibble at the tender leaves that hung from the trees. The Klobiodon they'd seen earlier was still wheeling through the sky. Tamiko couldn't help grinning. It was so amazing to see all these incredible animals she'd only ever read about, living and breathing and eating all around her. She couldn't quite believe she was really walking through the Jurassic!

Suddenly there was a ferocious rumble. Tamiko spun around.

A group of dinosaurs was prowling along the shore of the swamp. Unlike the four-legged

Cetiosauruses, these dinosaurs stood upright on muscular hind legs. They had huge claws that looked as sharp as daggers and they swung their large heads from side to side, scouting for prey. Their powerful tails thrashed behind them and their long teeth glinted in the sunlight. Tamiko's heart gave an unpleasant thump.

"Those guys look a lot meaner than the ones eating the trees," said Cheng.

"They're Allosauruses," said Tamiko. "The Cetiosauruses are herbivores, and just eat plants. But these are dangerous carnivores."

"Meat-eaters," said Cheng with a gulp.

Tamiko nodded. "Let's get out of here."

They were hurrying away, glancing

uneasily over their shoulders, when they heard a cry up ahead.

"What's that?" said Cheng.

They both stopped. Tamiko listened to the distant, high-pitched wail. It made her want to rush and help at once. "Whatever it is sounds pretty upset," she said.

"Maybe helping it is part of our mission," said Cheng. "Come on!"

Tamiko followed Cheng through the trees. They ducked beneath swinging clusters of ginkgo fruit and pushed through damp, curling ferns. The cries were getting closer.

They scrambled through a thicket of cycads into a small clearing. Tamiko gasped. A young dinosaur was sitting right in front of them. It had a round body, a little head, and two rows of bony plates jutting up all the way along its back. At the end of its tail was a cluster of spikes. The dinosaur was holding one of its front feet up in the air.

Tamiko gasped. "It's a baby Stegosaurus!"

The creature gave a pitiful wail.

"Is it a carnivore, too?" asked Cheng cautiously. "Like the Allosauruses?"

"Don't worry," said Tamiko. "Stegosaurs are herbivores." She walked slowly toward the crying dinosaur. "Where's your family, little one?"

"*Little one?*" Cheng said. "This guy must be more than six feet long!"

"That's nothing," said Tamiko with a grin. "Its mom and dad will be four times bigger!"

The baby Stegosaurus lifted its leathery head and cried again. Tamiko and Cheng looked around the clearing. There was no sign of the youngster's family.

"I wonder what's wrong with it," said Tamiko.

"I can see what's up," said Cheng. "Look—there's a thorn stuck in its foot."

Tamiko kneeled down to peer at the foot the Stegosaurus was holding up. Sticking into it was a long, mean-looking thorn. The Stegosaurus wailed again.

A distant rumble echoed across the plain.

"Uh oh," Tamiko said, glancing up. "That's the Allosauruses again. We've got to help this little guy, or they'll catch it."

Cheng reached for the thorn. His fingers were almost touching it when there was a whooshing sound. Cheng jumped back just in time to avoid the dinosaur's spiky tail as it crashed toward him.

"That wasn't very friendly," said Cheng. "We're trying to help you, buddy. We don't want you to be lunch for an Allosaurus."

The Stegosaurus thrashed its tail on the ground.

Tamiko had an idea. She searched around the clearing for some of the yellow ginkgo fruits, and reached up and plucked them.

"Now's not the time for a snack, Tamiko," said Cheng.

Tamiko laughed. "It's not for me," she said, twisting more fruit from the branches and filling her pockets. "It's for the

Stegosaurus. Here, take a handful."

Cheng took the fruit. He wrinkled his nose. "Ugh!" He shuddered. "It smells just like vomit!"

"I know," Tamiko said. "But I think the Stegosaurus will love it! If you distract it with the fruit, I might be able to pull the thorn out out of its foot."

Cheng waved the ginkgo under the little dinosaur's nose. "Here, baby Steg! Yummy, stinky ginkgo just for you!"

The dinosaur sniffed at the fruit. It opened its mouth to take a bite. Very slowly, Tamiko reached down and gripped the thorn. She gave it a swift tug—and out came the thorn!

"Got it!" she said, backing away to a safe distance.

The baby Stegosaurus gave a squeak of surprise. Ginkgo juice dribbled down its chin. Then it shook its foot, put it down on the ground, and trotted out of the clearing as if nothing had happened.

"Fantastic!" said Cheng. "Let's get back to hunting for that egg."

"I think we'd better check that the Stegosaurus finds its herd first,"

Tamiko said. "And make sure it isn't found by the Allosauruses..."

They pushed through the ginkgo branches. On a wide plain, a herd of adult Stegosauruses were grazing on some ferns. Tamiko caught her breath. They were even more incredible than she could have imagined! They blew through their nostrils like enormous cows as they pulled the ferns up by their roots. The crests of bony plates on their backs looked like armor.

Tamiko and Cheng stayed out of sight behind a ginkgo tree. They watched as the baby Stegosaurus stumbled up to a large adult and butted its leg with its head. The adult gave an affectionate-sounding rumble, and butted the little dinosaur back.

"That must be its mother," said Cheng. "For such a huge animal, I guess the baby's pretty cute."

One of the Stegosauruses suddenly raised its head. The rest of the herd did the same. Tamiko could sense the mood changing, from contentment to alarm. The mother Stegosaurus swished her enormous spiky tail and roared. Tamiko looked around, wondering what had spooked her.

Through the trees and ferns, she caught a flash of muscular legs and daggerlike talons. The air filled with a terrible rumble.

"Oh no!" gasped Tamiko.

The Allosauruses had arrived!

Chapter Three
A STINKY DISGUISE

"Hide!" Tamiko hissed.

She and Cheng dove behind a large clump of ferns. The ground shuddered as a large, scaly foot crashed down nearby. Deadly claws raked the mossy ground.

Tamiko counted eight scary Allosauruses prowling toward the Stegosaurus herd. They were enormous, with sharp, serrated teeth.

Long, razor-sharp claws gleamed on their forelimbs. Tamiko's throat felt dry and she and Cheng huddled close together.

The Stegosauruses roared at the attackers and thrashed their tails in warning. The Allosauruses roared back. The baby hid behind its mother's legs as the herd prepared to fight.

An Allosaurus darted in and nipped at the mother Stegosaurus. With surprising speed, the Stegosaurus's spiky tail thrashed down. One of the spikes caught the Allosaurus on the rump. It yelped with pain and quickly backed away.

"We need to leave," Cheng said, as an Allosaurus tail swished dangerously close to their fern clump. "If we get caught up in this fight, we'll never survive!"

One of the Allosauruses suddenly turned its head and sniffed the air. It had smelled something. Tamiko and Cheng shrank back.

"I really hope that isn't us it's sniffing," whispered Cheng.

The Allosaurus flared its nostrils as it swung its head about, searching... And Tamiko's stomach flipped as it looked right in their direction.

"It's smelled us!" Tamiko said in a tight voice.

Cheng gasped. "What do we do now?"

Tamiko looked around desperately. A short distance from their ferns was a pile of dark brown Allosaurus droppings.

"Disguise our scent," she said, and pointed at them.

Cheng's eyes widened. "You mean, cover ourselves in *dinosaur poop?*"

"It's either that, or get eaten," said Tamiko.

Cheng groaned. "And I thought the ginkgo fruit smelled bad!"

The dinosaurs were properly fighting now. The Allosauruses swung their massive heads, their jaws opened wide, while the Stegosauruses charged. Rumbles and grunts rang out. The Allosaurus that had spotted them twisted around and lunged at a passing Stegosaurus.

"Now!" Tamiko said. "While it's distracted!"

They wriggled on their bellies across the open plain. Tamiko felt as if every one of her muscles was tense. At any moment, an Allosaurus might close its jaws around her...

But they reached the heap of dino droppings without being caught. Tamiko grabbed two large fern leaves and handed one to Cheng. "Use this to smear it on," she said.

"Gross," said Cheng. But he scooped up

the Allosaurus poop and rubbed it on his arm. "This mission really stinks!"

The stench made Tamiko's eyes water. But it seemed to be working. Even though Tamiko and Cheng were lying close to the battle, the Allosauruses didn't seem to have noticed them.

"Now run," Tamiko ordered.

Not daring to look back, they sprinted across the plain, scrambling through ferns and across the spongy, mossy ground until they came to a steep hillside. Tamiko and Cheng clambered up, grabbing on to boulders to help them climb. High above them, they could see rows of tall conifers with dark branches that waved in the wind.

Tamiko pulled herself up onto a rocky ledge which jutted out a little from the hillside. She panted for breath and wiped her sweaty forehead. They'd made it to safety—for now.

"I wish it was so easy to escape the stink," Cheng said as he climbed up beside Tamiko. He was hot and panting from their climb. "Wow, some view!"

A wide green plain stretched away into the distance, broken by dense patches of trees. Tamiko could just make out tiny herds of grazing herbivores. Beyond a stretch of forest shimmered the swamp where they had left the Beagle.

A roar sounded close by—too close for comfort...

Tamiko and Cheng looked at each other

in dismay. "An Allosaurus," said Tamiko. "They're still close. We need to hide!"

They scrambled up a few more boulders and heaved themselves over a lip of rock. In front of them, looking a bit like an open mouth, was a cave. They darted inside. The craggy walls were high and wide, with water running down them. Moss grew in tufts on the ground.

It was cool and dark. Tamiko shivered.

"I'm glad we're safe," said Cheng, "but we really need to find that egg."

FIND THAT EGG, THAT EGG, THAT E-G-G-G... Cheng's voice echoed around the cave.

"Wow, that's spooky!" said Tamiko.

SPOO-OO-OOKY... said the echo.

"But cool," Cheng added with a grin. "In cave formations like this, where the roof is really high, the soundwaves bounce off the walls like rubber balls. We'd better whisper so the dinosaurs don't notice us."

"Thanks, Geology Explorer, said Tamiko".

EXPLORER-ER-ER-ER-ER, said the walls.

Tamiko explored a little deeper into the cave. The water running down the rock face was coming from an opening somewhere high above them. A pile of half-eaten bones littered one corner.

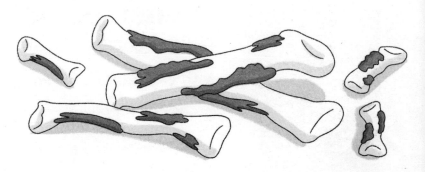

They peered out of the cave mouth, looking down the hillside to see if they could spot the Allosauruses coming after them. Movement caught Tamiko's eye—the branches of a conifer growing near the cave were swaying. Her chest tightened. *Have the Allosauruses found us?* she wondered.

The branches moved again and a strange bird emerged. It perched on the end of one of them. It was about the size of a crow, with a lizard-like head, a long bony tail, and sturdy legs. It spread its wings. Tamiko caught

a flash of white markings across black feathers.

"Wow!" gasped Tamiko. She was fizzing with excitement. "It's an Archaeopteryx!"

"An archae-what-eryx?" asked Cheng.

"It's somewhere between a dinosaur and a bird," explained Tamiko. "Birds evolved from dinosaurs. So even though Archaeopteryx is a dinosaur, it's developed some of the things you see in birds—like flight feathers and light bones so it can fly."

"Cool!" said Cheng. "But are you sure it's a dinosaur? It doesn't look like any of the others we've seen."

"I know," said Tamiko with a grin. "But it's got claws on its wings, and bones in its tail... Oh, and teeth! Look!"

The Archaeopteryx was snapping its beak at the conifer. *Probably pecking up insects,* Tamiko thought. Something was nestled in the crook of the branch—something round and pale... Her heart leaped.

"There's an egg!" she said, pointing it out to Cheng.

"Oh, yes!" cried Cheng. "Do you think it's the one from our mission?"

"I don't know," Tamiko said. Were they supposed to help the egg? It looked okay to her.

The Archaeopteryx stretched its feathery wings again. It seemed unsettled. Tamiko hoped that she and Cheng weren't upsetting it.

There was a cracking of broken branches, farther down the hillside. They heard a familiar roar, like a rumble of thunder.

"The Allosauruses are back!" said Tamiko. "No wonder the Archaeopteryx is worried."

Tamiko and Cheng ducked back into the cave. They peeped out nervously. Four Allosauruses had made it up the hillside and were prowling through the conifers below them, sniffing and roaring. One of them snapped its jaws at the Archaeopteryx. The Archaeopteryx shrieked and took off, gliding away through the trees.

Her egg was left all alone on the branch.

Tamiko and Cheng looked at each other.

"This is our mission," Tamiko said. "We've got to save that egg!"

Chapter Four
PTEROSAUR TERROR

The wind blew, shaking the conifer. The egg wobbled, but stayed tucked into the crook of the branch. It was a little smaller than a hen's egg.

"This isn't good," Tamiko said. She scanned the sky. "If the mother doesn't come back, the egg will be in trouble."

The Allosauruses prowled on through the

conifers. Tamiko and Cheng listened as the sound of cracking branches grew quieter. When the Allosauruses were far enough away, they settled close to the mouth of the cave to keep watch for the Archaeopteryx.

The cave went completely dark as a huge leathery wing blocked out the light. Tamiko and Cheng drew back. It was Ramphorynchus, another type of pterosaur—a huge one! It landed on a branch in front of the cave mouth, which groaned and buckled beneath its weight. It flapped its gigantic wings to keep its balance.

Tamiko laughed at the astonished look on Cheng's face. "It's... so... huge," he said.

"The biggest pterosaur fossil ever found was from an animal called Quetzalcoatlus. It had a wingspan of about 36 feet from tip to tip," she said. "Quetzalcoatlus was the largest flying creature ever!"

EVER... EVER... EVER echoed the cave. The pterosaur's head swung around toward the noise. It stared into the cave mouth—straight at Tamiko and Cheng.

"It's seen us," said Cheng, shuffling backward as quickly as he could.

The large pterosaur swooped down from the branch and dive-bombed the cave mouth, snapping its long

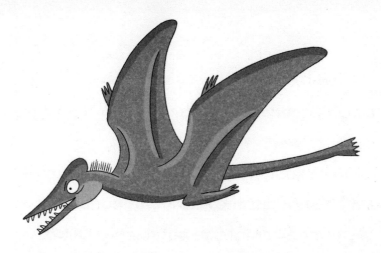

beak. Tamiko felt the brush of a leathery wing tip against her leg as she scrambled back into the cave.

"Whoa!" she gasped.

The pterosaur screeched and swooped again. Its massive wings clattered against the rockface as it tried to fit inside the cave.

Tamiko and Cheng huddled at the back. Tamiko's heart was racing, but she couldn't help gazing at the pterosaur in awe. *I can't believe I'm this close to an actual living one!* she thought. Inside its long, snapping beak she could see teeth.

"We've got to make it go away," Cheng said. "Otherwise we'll be stuck in this stinky cave forever!"

Tamiko sniffed. "You're right, it does stink. And it's not just the Allosaurus poop..." Then she remembered! She put her hand into her pocket and pulled out a handful of ginkgo fruits. "I've got an idea..."

Pulling back her arm, Tamiko lobbed the yellow fruit as far as she could. It sailed away into the conifers. With a shriek, the pterosaur soared after the fruit and disappeared into the trees.

"Nice one," said Cheng, sounding a little shaky. "Let's take a closer look at the egg."

They hurried over to the Archaeopteryx's conifer. Luckily, the egg was still sitting safely on its branch.

Cheng shaded his eyes as he looked up at the sky. "I can't see the mother anywhere," he said.

The egg gave a funny shiver. Tamiko peered more closely at it. *Maybe it's about to hatch*, she thought with a rush of excitement.

There was a rumbling under her feet. The earth shifted and groaned.

It wasn't the *egg* that was moving. It was the *ground*!

"Earthquake!" Tamiko gasped. There were lots of earthquakes at Tamiko's home in Japan. She recognized the signs.

The ground rocked again. Cheng flung out his arm to steady himself against the trunk of a nearby tree. The conifer branches shivered and shook. The egg rocked back and forth... then it tipped over and plunged toward the ground.

"Oh no!" Tamiko gasped.

She flung herself toward the falling egg, stretching out her arms. The egg fell neatly into her hands.

"Yes!" Cheng shouted.

But the earth gave a terrible groan. A long, dark crack zigzagged through the shaking trees.

"I don't like the look of that," said Cheng. He pointed at a trickle of water coming up through the ground. "Rising water is a really bad sign. And the rumbling is getting louder. That's not good either."

Tamiko clasped the egg to her chest.

"What's happening?" she asked. Tamiko wasn't sure she wanted to know the answer.

Cheng looked grim. "There's about to be a landslide. RUN!"

The ground bucked and tipped. Suddenly it was almost impossible for Tamiko to keep her balance. Rocks rained around them, and falling branches crashed past their heads. Tamiko felt the earth sliding away beneath her feet. She tripped, and landed hard on her bottom.

"Whoa!" she cried as she slid down the slipping hillside.

She could see Cheng surfing the tumbling earth beside her, crouched low to keep his balance. She held the egg close to her chest and curled her arms around it. *I've got to keep the egg safe...*

They bumped and slid down the hillside. Stones bounced around, hitting Tamiko painfully on her arms and shins. Cheng crashed down the hill on his stomach with his arms stretched out in front of him.

After what seemed like forever, the shaking hillside grew quieter and the earthquake stopped.

Cheng got to his feet and ran over to Tamiko. There was dirt in his hair and twigs snagged in his clothing. "Are you OK? Is the egg...?"

Tamiko uncurled her arms very carefully to reveal the egg. She grinned with relief at the sight of the unbroken shell. "It's fine,"

she said. "Thanks to your geology expertise! If we hadn't run, we'd all have been crushed." She got to her feet. "But the mother Archaeopteryx will have no idea where her egg is. We've got to get it back up that tree."

They both looked up at the collapsed hillside. Boulders were scattered at strange angles. Broken trees lay across the steep, uneven earth. At the top of the hill, the Archaeopteryx's tree was still standing. But

Tamiko could see that it was impossible to climb up the shattered hillside.

"We'll have to find another way up," she said. "We'll walk around until—oh!"

The egg was moving in her hands. A tiny crack appeared in the spotted shell. Tamiko sank back on to the ground, staring as the egg shook and shivered with life.

"Cheng," she said. "I think the baby Archaeopteryx is hatching!"

Chapter Five
DINO DINNERTIME

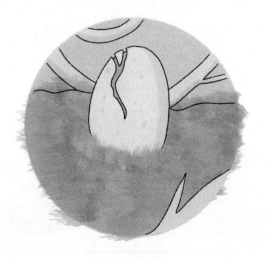

Tamiko couldn't believe she was about to see a dinosaur hatch! She spotted a clump of soft moss and gently settled the egg into it.

She and Cheng kneeled beside it. The egg cracked open a little more. Then a piece of shell fell away and a tiny creature pushed its way out. Tamiko thought it looked exactly like a mix of a bird and a lizard. It had scrawny feathers and bright, curious eyes.

"Amazing!" she murmured.

The baby Archaeopteryx fluffed out its tiny feathers, opened its jaws and squawked.

"I think it's hungry," said Cheng.

Worry fluttered inside Tamiko. She knew all about fossilized dinosaurs, but she had no idea how to take care of a living one.

The Archaeopteryx squawked again and opened its jaws, as if it expected Tamiko and Cheng to drop some food inside them.

"We need help," Tamiko said. "Let's ask the Secret Explorers how we should take care of it."

Tamiko pulled up a clump of moss and lined the pocket on the front of her hoodie with it. Then she carefully scooped up the baby Archaeopteryx and tucked it inside.

She noticed that it still had a piece of shell stuck to its wing, and she couldn't resist tucking it into her jeans pocket as a souvenir.

They set off for the swamp where they'd parked the Beagle. They passed the clearing where they had found the baby Stegosaurus, and hurried through the ferns and drooping ginkgo branches.

As they approached the swamp, they heard screeching. The Beagle was covered in little pterosaurs! They were flapping their leathery wings and squawking at each other.

KRAAA! KRAAA! KRAAA! screeched the pterosaurs.

KRRR-P! PIPP-PPP! the Beagle beeped back. It sounded very angry.

Tamiko laughed. "I think the Beagle's trying to tell them to go away! Go on, shoo!" she called, running toward them and waving her arms.

The pterosaurs flew off, and the Beagle gave a satisfied beep.

Cheng jumped into one of the seats and tapped a screen on the dashboard. "I hope this works," he said. "We're one hundred and fifty million years away from home..." He switched on a microphone. "Calling Exploration Station! Exploration Station, come in!"

The screen flickered. The faces of the other Secret Explorers appeared, all gathered around a screen.

"Hi, guys!" said Connor. "How's it going in the Jurassic?"

"Apart from being swatted at by a Stegosaurus and covered in Allosaurus poop," said Cheng, "it's going well!"

"And we've got a new member of the team to introduce to you," said Tamiko. She put her hand into the pocket of her hoodie and drew out the little Archaeopteryx. It flapped its tiny wings.

"Whoa!" said Roshni. "Is that a baby dinosaur?"

"It's an Archaeopteryx." Tamiko quickly explained what had happened. "So we need to take it back to where its mother will find it, but in the meantime we've got no idea how to look after it."

Leah the Biology Explorer was frowning thoughtfully. "I don't know how to care for a baby Archaeopteryx," she said. "But if it's anything like taking care of a bird's chick, I can help. First, you need to keep it warm."

Tamiko showed her the bed of moss inside her pocket.

"Perfect!" said Leah. "You should feed it grubs, beetles, insects, and worms."

"Do they have those in the Jurassic?" wondered Ollie.

"There are actually more insects around than dinosaurs," Tamiko said. "Beetles, dragonflies, and wasps all lived during the Jurassic Period. And there are worms all over the place, too!"

"That's great," said Leah. "Oh, and don't look at the Archaeopteryx for too long."

"Why not?" asked Cheng. "Will we scare it, or something?"

"It might think you're its parents," Leah explained. "And then it won't accept its real mother."

Tamiko and Cheng thanked their friends for their help.

"Good luck!" called Kiki, and they all waved goodbye. Cheng switched off the screen and Tamiko tucked the Archaeopteryx back into her pocket. It gave her finger a sharp nip.

"Ow!" she said. "Cheng, we really need to find some baby dino food."

They set off in the direction of what was left of the hillside. As they walked, they scanned the ground and the tree branches for anything the Archaeopteryx might like to eat. Cheng

spotted a dead beetle on a fern leaf and scooped it up.

"It's called Brochocoleus," Tamiko said.

"Otherwise known as... dinner!" said Cheng.

He dangled the beetle in front of Tamiko's hoodie pocket. The Archaeopteryx poked its head out. With one snap of its jaws, the beetle disappeared.

"I think it enjoyed that!" said Cheng with a grin. "Hey, is that a worm?"

They trekked around the base of the hillside, picking up the insects and worms they spotted and feeding them to the Archaeopteryx. It gulped everything down, flapping its little wings.

"Whoa," said Cheng, as they stepped onto a lush, grassy plain. "What are THEY?"

A group of truly enormous dinosaurs were reaching up with their long necks to graze on the topmost branches of the trees. They swished their huge tails in the long grass.

"They're Turiasauruses," said Tamiko, gazing at the herd in wonder. They were even larger than she had imagined. "They're the biggest dinosaurs ever found in Europe. Scientists believe that just one Turiasaurus was the weight of six or seven elephants."

"Wow," said Cheng. "Hey!" He pointed to a plume of steam rising from the other side of the plain. "It looks like we're heading for a geothermal spring. The water will be nice and warm— so we can wash off the Allosaurus poop!"

They hurried across the grass until they reached a stony area with a large, shallow pool of water. Steam looped and swirled in the air. Tamiko took off her hoodie and put it gently down on the warm ground, with the baby Archaeopteryx snuggled into the fabric. Then she waded into the spring with the rest of her clothes on. The heat seeped through her jeans, lifting off the dried Allosaurus poop and heating her skin. "It's as warm as a real bath!" she said.

Cheng also sank up to his neck in the bubbling water. He dunked his head and rubbed the dirt and dinosaur dung from his face. "The water's being heated up by magma," he explained. "That's hot liquid rock below the Earth's crust."

Once they were nice and clean, they dried themselves with large handfuls of moss and Tamiko slipped her hoodie back over her head. She stroked the Archaeopteryx with one finger, careful to follow Leah's instructions and not look at it for too long.

"Let's take you home, OK?" she said.

Tamiko and Cheng continued around

the bottom of the collapsed hillside. They scrambled over rocks and pushed through thick branches—until they reached a deep crack in the ground. It was deep and too wide for them to jump. It stretched away from them in both directions, wriggling across the landscape like a giant snake.

"There's no way across," said Cheng with dismay.

What were they going to do?

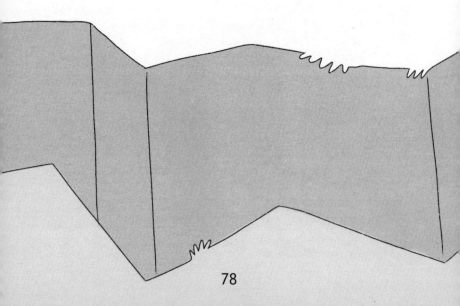

Chapter Six
RACE TO THE NEST

"The crack must have been caused by the earthquake," Cheng said. He knelt down and scooped up a handful of soil. "This ground has only just been disturbed."

"The crack must end somewhere," Tamiko said. She started walking along it. "For all we know, the mother Archaeopteryx could already be back in her conifer, wondering where her egg has gone. We've got to get her baby back to her!"

They hurried along. Some trees had fallen down, uprooted by the earthquake. Ahead of them a large boulder slid into the crack. It felt like forever before Tamiko and Cheng heard it land at the bottom.

"This is no good," Tamiko said, after ten minutes of walking. They still couldn't see the end of the crack. "Let's try the other direction."

They turned back. As they walked, Cheng lifted worms and bugs from broken clods of earth for the hungry little dinosaur.

"I don't think this crack is ever going to end," he said, peering up ahead.

Tamiko groaned. This was taking way too long. She sat down on a fallen tree to think... and an idea struck her. She jumped up. "We can use this tree to make a bridge!"

"Good idea," said Cheng. "In theory."

Tamiko put her hands on her hips. "What do you mean, *in theory*?"

"It's massive," said Cheng. "We'll never be able to move it."

He had a point. The tree was enormous, with a thick trunk and huge branches.

"But we could look for a smaller one," Cheng added.

Broken trees lay around them like spilled matches. Tamiko took off her hoodie once more and left the Archaeopteryx inside it, enjoying a worm. Then she and Cheng clambered around the fallen tree, searching for the perfect bridge. They tried to lift one or two of the smaller ones, but couldn't get a grip. Their best find was a small, stout ginkgo tree which lay near the deep crack.

Together, they rolled the broken tree across the ground.

"Let's both keep hold of one end," Tamiko said," and push it across the crack."

They both held onto one end of the trunk and shuffled it along. Earth fell away as the trunk inched over the edge of the crack. Clods thumped into the darkness below. Finally, the far end of the trunk touched down on the other side. Tamiko and Cheng cheered.

"Nice work, teammate!" said Tamiko, grinning.

Something brushed past her ankles, making her jump. She glanced down to see a Compsognathus hurtle past her. A whole group of the little carnivores sprinted out from a clump of ferns, screeching and snapping their teeth.

"The Archaeopteryx!" Tamiko cried. "They'll eat it!"

She ran toward the Compsognathuses, waving her arms. "Go away!" she shouted. Cheng joined in, waving a broken branch. The scavengers had reached Tamiko's hoodie. She raced through them and scooped the baby Archaeopteryx into her arms.

The Compsognathuses circled around her legs. Cheng waved his branch and yelled at the top of his voice. "Go and eat something else!" he told them.

Still screeching, as if they were disappointed, the little dinosaurs darted away.

"We'd better get over our bridge before they come back," said Tamiko. Her heart was still hammering.

Cradling the Archaeopteryx, Tamiko walked across the tree-trunk bridge as quickly as she dared. The rocky darkness below her yawned like a hungry mouth that would gobble her up if she slipped. Tamiko's knees trembled. **Don't look down**, she told herself. She jumped off on the other side.

Cheng puffed out his cheeks. Then he

took the bridge at a run. As he leaped down beside Tamiko he gasped with relief. "Phew! We made it."

They scrambled and clambered as best they could up the hill, gripping on to boulders and branches as they went. Tamiko could see the conifers at the top. "We'll soon have you home again," she told the Archaeopteryx. As they climbed, Cheng found beetles and worms that the dinosaur gulped down.

At last, they made it up to the trees. "So which one was it?" said Cheng.

Tamiko studied the conifers before them. A few had fallen in the landslide. She pointed at one that was a little taller than the others, with dark green, strongly scented needles. "That one, I think," she said.

They listened for the cries of the mother Archaeopteryx. But they could only hear the rustling of the branches. Tamiko chewed her lip with worry.

"What if she doesn't come back?" said Cheng.

"Let's gather food that she'll like and put it in the tree," Tamiko suggested. "That might attract her back."

They hunted around for a few more worms and beetles. Tamiko suddenly remembered the pile of bones inside the cave. She darted in and fetched them—they still had shreds of meat on them for the mother dinosaur to eat.

"This might do it!" she called as she came back out.

DO IT... DO IT... DO IT... went the echo.

Cheng was climbing the tree, pulling himself up through the branches. He crouched on a branch just below where the egg had rested. He reached down and Tamiko passed up the food. Cheng laid it on the branch above his head. "A delicious banquet," he said. "Well, it is if you happen to be an Archaeopteryx."

Tamiko heard a snuffling

sound. She looked around and saw that the Stegosaurus herd was back. They were grazing on the ferns that grew in the gaps between the trees. The baby Stegosaurus made its way up through the conifers and snuffled around Tamiko. In its mouth was a big fern leaf it was chewing on. It peered up at Cheng sitting in the tree and grunted.

"I think it wants to know what we're doing," Tamiko said, laughing.

The fern fell out of the little Stegosaurus's mouth. Tamiko saw its nostrils flare. It gave a frightened whimper. At once, the adults started bellowing as well.

"What's up with them?" asked Cheng.

Tamiko felt cold all over. She thought she knew... and sure enough, a familiar roar reached them through the trees.

Tamiko and Cheng looked at each other in alarm.

"The Allosauruses are back!" cried Tamiko.

Chapter Seven

TAMIKO-RAPTOR

The Stegosaurus herd thundered away, snorting and bellowing.

Everything went very quiet.

"I don't like this," said Cheng. He slid quickly down the tree.

Tamiko's panicked breath was loud in her ears. The silence was unbearable. Where were the Allosauruses?

Cheng sniffed his arms sadly. "I wish we hadn't washed off the poop now," he muttered. "The Allosauruses will definitely smell us this time."

Tamiko clenched her fists, and forced herself to think calmly. "We've got two problems," she said. "First, the mother Archaeopteryx will never come back if she knows the Allosauruses are nearby. And second, if they find us they will definitely eat us!"

More roars sounded through the trees. "And we haven't got long to solve them."

"What about the cave?" Cheng said. "We could hide there."

Tamiko glanced over at the dark cave mouth. It did look tempting... But she shook her head. "If we go in there, the Allosauruses will have us trapped with no way out."

Cheng's eyes gleamed. "I know! We can use the cave, but not to hide inside—we can use the echo! If we yell really loudly, maybe it'll scare the Allosauruses away."

"You mean, roar at the dinosaurs?" Tamiko felt a stir of hope. "Like we're dinosaurs, too?"

Cheng grinned. "Exactly!"

The baby Archaeopteryx squawked. Tamiko tickled the little dinosaur under its jaw. "I think it likes the idea," she said. "Let's try it!"

The roars were even closer now. Tamiko stuffed handfuls of moss into a hollow in the trunk of one of the conifers, and placed the little dinosaur inside. If their plan didn't work, at least the Archaeopteryx would be okay. It blinked at her.

"Stay safe," said Tamiko. "Don't make any noise, OK?"

The Archaeopteryx snuggled into the moss, folding its wings tightly around itself.

Tamiko and Cheng dashed into the cave. "Let's head for the back," said Cheng. "The echoes will be loudest there."

As soon as they crouched down in the shadows, the Allosauruses came crashing through the trees just outside the cave.

Tamiko could see their powerful leg muscles flexing as they prowled, grunting and bellowing at each other. They sniffed the trees and the rocks. Tamiko gripped Cheng's arm tightly as the predators came closer and closer to the cave...

The biggest Allosaurus flared its nostrils. It lowered its head, sniffing the entrance to the cave—then roared. "It knows we're here," whispered Tamiko. Her heart was racing.

If this doesn't work, she thought, *we're Allosaurus dinner!*

"Ready?" Cheng whispered.

"Ready," whispered Tamiko. "On three. One... two..."

"RRAAAARGHHH!!!!" Tamiko and Cheng screamed, at the top of their lungs.

RRRARRRRARRRARRRGHARGGHARGHH! roared the echo. The sound seemed to swoop around the cave. It was so loud, Tamiko and

Cheng covered their ears.

"RRRARRRGH!" they yelled again. "RRARRRRRGH!"

RRRARRRRRARGHARGGHARGHH… RRRARRRRARRRARRRGHARGGHARGHH… RRRARRRRARRRARRRGHARGGHARGHH!

As he roared, Cheng curled his fingers as if they were claws and stalked around, pretending to be a dinosaur. Despite the danger, Tamiko couldn't help giggling. *RRRARRRRARRRARRRGHARGGHARGHH!*

HEEHAHEEHAHEEHEEEEE! The echo of Tamiko's laughter sounded very spooky.

The Allosaurus skittered back from the cave mouth. It tilted its head, and Tamiko wondered if it was trying to figure out what kind of dinosaur would make such a strange noise. With a snarl, it retreated.

Very, very quietly, Tamiko and Cheng crept to the mouth of the cave and peered out.

The big Allosaurus was lumbering away from the cave, and down the hillside. The rest of the predators   followed, their   heads   held

low. The echoes had really scared them!

"Hooray!" cried Tamiko. "We did it!"

"Just call me Ty-Cheng-osaurus rex!" said Cheng, laughing. "And you're a Tamiko-raptor!"

Now the Allosauruses had finally left. But would the mother Archaeopteryx come back?

Chapter Eight
FLYING HOME

Tamiko and Cheng were sitting in one of the other conifer trees, scanning the Jurassic sky for the Archaeopteryx mother. Pterosaurs circled and they could hear the trumpeting calls of dinosaurs grazing on the plain below.

But there was no sign anywhere of the mother dinosaur.

They took turns to scavenge for worms and bugs to feed the baby Archaeopteryx. It was back on the branch where it had rested inside its egg, squawking and fussing its feathers with its tiny jaws.

The sun began slowly to sink.

"What if the mother never comes back?" Cheng asked anxiously.

Tamiko rubbed her eyes. "I don't know," she admitted. She didn't want to think about that possibility.

Cheng eyed the worm wriggling in Tamiko's hand. "I'm so hungry, I could eat that myself," he said.

Tamiko went over to the Archaeopteryx, and dropped the worm into its open jaws. "Too late," she said.

The sky was turning to gold now. Cheng leaned against the trunk with his arms across his knees. "I'm going to sit here and dream about spaghetti," he said. "A nice big bowl of spaghetti and meatballs. And ice cream for dessert. And—what?"

Tamiko had lifted her hand. She stared into the sky. "Listen," she said.

The baby Archaeopteryx squawked excitedly. Away in the distance, Tamiko and Cheng heard an answering cry. It wasn't the piercing scream of a pterosaur, or the snuffling of a Stegosaurus. It wasn't the roar of an Allosaurus either.

"There!" Tamiko exclaimed. "Cheng, look! It's the mom! She's come at last!"

Swooping through the golden sky, they saw the mother Archaeopteryx. Her wings were spread wide. Her baby cried, and she

answered. Tamiko and Cheng watched as she circled the conifers.

She dropped onto a branch beside it. Tamiko glimpsed a wriggling beetle in her jaws. In the next instant it had gone, straight down the baby's throat.

Tamiko and Cheng looked at each other. Doing their best not to scare the mother away again, they both silently punched the air.

More cries circled overhead. Four more adult Archaeopteryxes descended from the golden clouds. They settled beside the baby.

"It's an Archaeopteryx habitat!" Tamiko whispered. "Cheng, we haven't just saved one Archaeopteryx from the Allosauruses. We've saved thousands."

"There's only five," Cheng pointed out. "Six if you include the baby."

"There are only six right now," said Tamiko. "But thanks to us these guys can settle here without worrying about predators. They can thrive, and have more babies. And those babies will have babies, and THOSE babies will have babies for a thousand generations—and THAT plays a part in the whole evolution of modern birds!"

"Whoa," exclaimed Cheng, impressed. "I guess we deserve a pat on the back after all."

Tamiko could have stayed forever, watching the Archaeopteryxes circle and squawk. But the Beagle was waiting for them back at the swamp. So was the team at the Exploration Station, waiting for news of their mission. They made their way slowly and carefully back down the shattered hillside, and picked their way through the trees and ferns. They made it to the edge of the swamp as the Jurassic sun began to dip below the horizon.

They got in and buckled their seatbelts. Tamiko pressed the HOME button on the Beagle's handlebars. There was a grind of gears, a whoosh of wind, and a flash of light. Tamiko felt the soft leather seat change back to familiar, splintered wood. Then finally they were back in the Exploration Station.

"That was a close call!" said Leah. "We've been following the whole thing."

Everyone gathered around Tamiko and Cheng, chattering and laughing and congratulating them on their successful mission.

"Did you bring anything back?" Ollie asked.

Tamiko remembered the little souvenir she had kept. She put her hand into her pocket and drew out a piece of the Archaeopteryx egg. But instead of a delicate piece of shell, it had transformed into a rock.

"It's a fossil now!" she exclaimed, studying the little fragment in astonishment.

"One hundred and fifty million years will do that," said Gustavo with a grin.

Tamiko opened one of the glass display cases. She placed her eggshell next to a fossilized shark's tooth and gently shut the door.

"I enjoyed that, Tamiko," said Cheng. "Apart from the Allosauruses. Oh, and the poop!"

Tamiko and Cheng bumped fists and smiled at each other. And then, after waving at the others, Tamiko stepped through the glowing door.

There was a flash of light, and a jolt. Tamiko thrust out her hand to steady herself in the fierce blast of wind. Her fingers touched the warm, painted surface of a doorframe.

She was back in Nemuro, outside her favorite fossil shop again.

"Oh!" she gasped.

A perfectly fossilized feather sat in the fossil shop window, caught forever in a slice of rock. Tamiko closed her eyes, remembering the feel of the warm, straggly baby dinosaur in her pocket. She grinned.

Her mission had been awesome. And she couldn't *wait* for her next one!

DINOSAUR TIMELINE

The time when dinosaurs dominated the Earth is called the Mesozoic Era. It lasted for over 180 million years. This era is divided into three time periods called the Triassic, Jurassic, and Cretaceous. During these periods, the climate changed and different plants and animals appeared.

TRIASSIC PERIOD

Most of the Earth was hot and dry. There weren't many plants and the land was a desert. Small dinosaurs and tiny mammals began to appear for the first time.

250–200 million years ago

Plateosaur

Eoraptor

Coelophysis

TAMIKO'S MISSION NOTES

JURASSIC PERIOD

The Earth became much wetter. Forests and lush vegetation grew, providing food for enormous plant-eating dinosaurs. Dragonflies and the first birds also appeared.

CRETACEOUS PERIOD

The temperature dropped, creating a warm, wet climate. Dinosaurs were the most powerful creatures on Earth— but at the end of the Cretaceous, many of them became extinct.

200–145 million years ago

145–66 million years ago

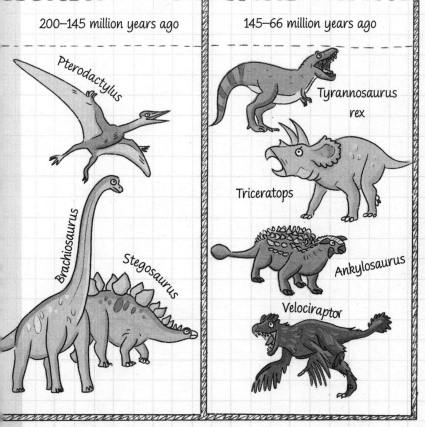

Pterodactylus

Brachiosaurus

Stegosaurus

Tyrannosaurus rex

Triceratops

Ankylosaurus

Velociraptor

WHO'S THAT DINO?

Our mission took us back in time to the Jurassic.
Here are some of the dinosaurs we met...

Allosaurus
(al-oh-Sore-uss)

Fearsome predator with dozens of sharp, serrated teeth. It hunted herbivores, such as Stegosaurus, as well as smaller predators.

- Size: 39 ft (12 m) long
- Habitat: Open woodlands
- Diet: Meat

Big skull

Muscular tail for balance

Archaeopteryx
(ar-kee-OP-ter-ix)

One of the oldest members of the bird family. The discovery of Archaeopteryx proved there is a link between dinosaurs and birds.

Jaws with teeth, like a dinosaur

- Size: 1.5 ft (45 cm) long
- Habitat: Forests
- Diet: Insects and reptiles

Feathers and wings, like a bird

- Size: 30 ft (9 m) long
- Habitat: Forests
- Diet: Plants

Stegosaurus (STEG-oh-SORE-uss)

A big plant-eater with a spiky tail for fighting off predators. It was the size of an elephant, but its brain was only the size of an apple!

Plates may have been brightly colored

NOT a dinosaur!

As well as the dinosaurs, plesiosaurs and pterosaurs lived during the Jurassic and Cretaceous Periods. Plesiosaurs lived in the oceans—they were giant meat-eaters with very long necks. Pterosaurs were flying reptiles, and included Pterodactylus.

Head crest made of toughened skin

Wings made of stretchy skin and muscle

HOW A FOSSIL IS MADE

Fossils are the remains of things that have been dead for millions of years. All sorts of life forms have fossilized, from spectacular Stegosaurus skeletons to tiny ammonite shells. Fossils help us understand how life on our planet has changed over millions of years. Scientists called paleontologists dig up and study fossils.

STEP 1 A creature dies and its body sinks into the mud by a river.

STEP 2 The creature is buried in layers of mud, sand, and ash over a period of millions of years.

STEP 3 The skeleton of the creature turns from bone to stone.

STEP 4 The fossilized creature is uncovered by paleontologists. They dig out the fossil and coat it in plaster to protect it. The fossil is then sent to a laboratory to be studied or to a museum to be displayed.

Types of fossil

* Body fossils, such as bones, teeth, and shells

* Petrified fossils, which are soft tissues, such as muscle and leaves

* Trace fossils, such as fossilized footprints, which tell scientists about a creature's behavior

* Coprolites—fossilized poops!

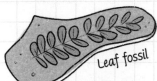

Leaf fossil

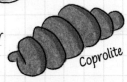

Coprolite

QUIZ

1   True or false: The time when the dinosaurs existed was called the Mesozoic Era.

2   Which period did Stegosaurus live in?

3   Which creature is a link between dinosaurs and birds?

4   True or false: Pterosaurs and Plesiosaurs are types of dinosaurs.

5   What is the name of a scientist who studies dinosaurs?

6   What is a coprolite?

7   How long ago did dinosaurs become extinct?

8   What did an Allosaurus eat?

SEARCH FOR DRAGONFLIES!

There are eight hidden dragonflies to spot in this book. Can you find them all?

They look like this!

Check your answers on page 127

GLOSSARY

AMMONITE
A type of sea creature that lived during the time of the dinosaurs

CARNIVORE
An animal that only eats meat

CONIFER
A cone-bearing tree with small needles

COPROLITE
Animal poop that has become fossilized

CRETACEOUS PERIOD
The third period of the Mesozoic Era (145–66 million years ago)

DINOSAUR
Prehistoric reptiles that lived during the Mesozoic Era

FOSSIL
Remains of a living thing that have become preserved in rock over time

FOSSILIZATION
The process of an animal or plant becoming a fossil

GINKGO
A type of tree that dates back to the Jurassic Period

HERBIVORE
An animal that only eats plant matter

JURASSIC PERIOD
The second period of the Mesozoic Era (200–145 million years ago)

MESOZOIC ERA
The time when dinosaurs lived— made up from the Triassic, Jurassic, and Cretaceous Periods

OMNIVORE
An animal that eats both plant matter and meat

PALEONTOLOGIST
A scientist who studies dinosaurs and other fossils

PLESIOSAUR
Marine reptile (usually with long necks) that lived during the Mesozoic Era

PREDATOR
An animal that hunts other animals for food

PTEROSAUR
Flying reptile that lived during the Mesozoic Era

REPTILES
Cold-blooded animals with scaly skin such as lizards, snakes, crocodiles, and dinosaurs

TRIASSIC PERIOD
The first period of the Mesozoic Era (250–200 million years ago)

Quiz answers

1. True

2. The Jurassic

3. Archaeopteryx

4. False

5. Paleontologist

6. Fossilized poop

7. 66 million years ago

8. Meat

For Oscar

Text for DK by Working Partners Ltd
9 Kingsway, London WC2B 6XF
With special thanks to Lucy Courtenay

Design by Collaborate Ltd
Illustrator Ellie O'Shea
Consultant Emily Keeble

Acquisitions Editor Sam Priddy
Senior Commissioning Designer Joanne Clark
US Senior Editor Shannon Beatty
Senior Production Editor Nikoleta Parasaki
Senior Producer Ena Matagic
Publishing Director Sarah Larter

First American Edition, 2020
Published in the United States by DK Publishing
1450 Broadway, Suite 801, New York, New York 10018

Text copyright © Working Partners Ltd 2020
Layout, illustration, and design copyright © 2020 Dorling
Kindersley Limited
DK, a Division of Penguin Random House LLC
20 21 22 23 24 10 9 8 7 6 5 4 3 2 1
001–318844–Oct/2020
All rights reserved.

A catalog record for this book is available from the
Library of Congress.

ISBN: 978-0-7440-2108-0 (Paperback)
ISBN: 978-0-7440-2387-9 (Hardcover)

Printed and bound in Great Britain by
Clays Ltd, Elcograf S.p.A.

For the curious
www.dk.com

The publisher would like to thank: Sally Beets, James Mitchem, and Seeta Parmar
for editorial assistance; and Caroline Twomey for proofreading.